NOTE

Dr. Clement C. Moore was born
in New York in 1779.
He was a Professor of Hebrew
and Greek but, today, his name
is remembered as the writer
of this poem.
Composed in 1822 for his six
children, it was first published
as "A Visit from St. Nicholas"
in 1823 and has since been
translated into many languages
including Braille.

First published in Great Britain 1980 by Award Publications Limited
© Award Publications Limited MCMLXXX

This edition is published by Derrydale Books,
a division of Crown Publishers, Inc.
by arrangement with Award Publications Limited

gh

Printed in Belgium

THE NIGHT BEFORE CHRISTMAS

by
Clement C. Moore L.L.D.

Illustrated by
RENE CLOKE

DERRYDALE BOOKS — NEW YORK

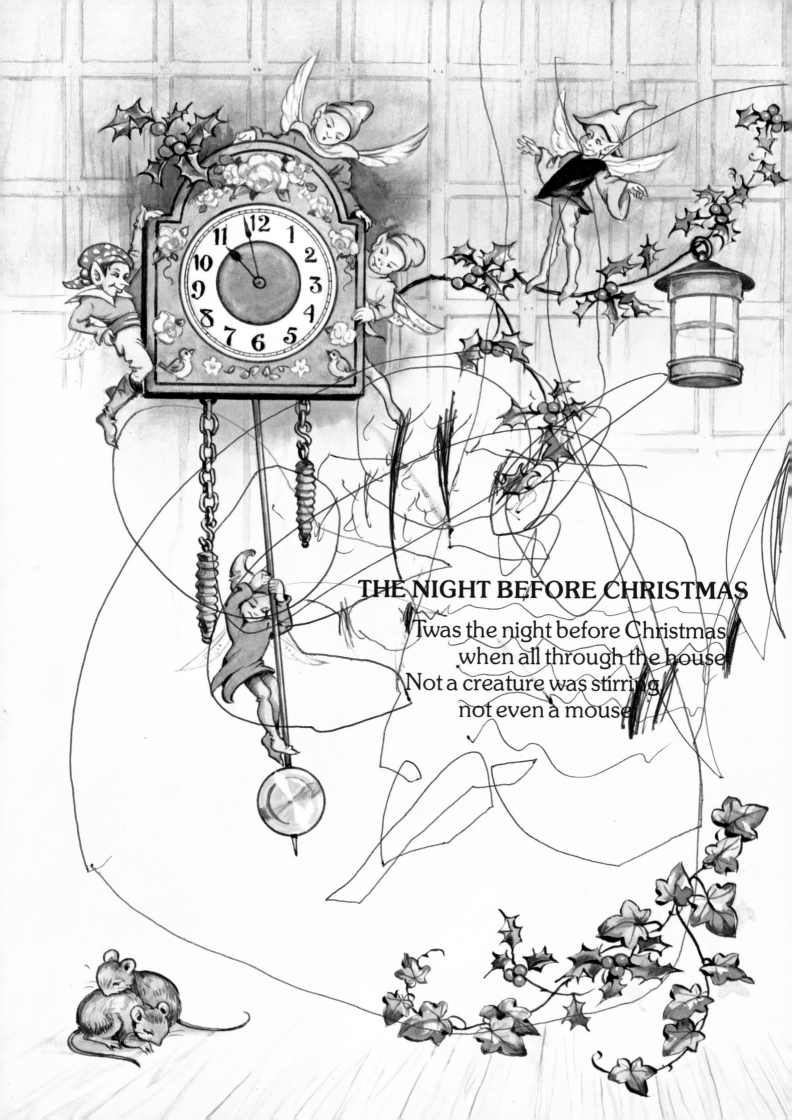

THE NIGHT BEFORE CHRISTMAS

Twas the night before Christmas
when all through the house
Not a creature was stirring,
not even a mouse.

The stockings were hung by the chimney with care,
In hopes that St. Nicholas soon would be there;

The children were nestled all snug in their beds,

While visions of sugar-plums
danced in their heads;

And Mamma in her kerchief,
and I in my cap,
Had just settled our brains
for a long winter's nap;

When out on the lawn
    there arose such a clatter,
I sprang from the bed
    to see what was the matter.

Away to the window
I flew like a flash,
Tore open the shutters and threw up the sash.

The moon on the breast
of the new-fallen snow,
Gave the lustre of midday to objects below;

When, what to my wondering eyes should appear,
But a miniature sleigh and eight tiny reindeer,
With a little old driver, so lively and quick,
I knew in a moment it must be St. Nick.

More rapid than eagles his coursers they came,
    And he whistled, and shouted, and called them by name:
"Now, Dasher! now, Dancer!
    now, Prancer and Vixen!
On, Comet! on, Cupid!
    on, Donner and Blitzen!

To the top of the porch!
     to the top of the wall!
Now dash away! dash away!
     dash away all!''
As dry leaves that before
     the wild hurricane fly,
When they meet with an obstacle,
     mount to the sky,
So up to the house-top
     the coursers they flew,
With the sleigh full of toys,
     and St. Nicholas too.

And then, in a twinkling, I heard on the roof
The prancing and pawing
of each little hoof.

As I drew in my head, and was turning around,
Down the chimney St. Nicholas
came with a bound.

He was dressed all in fur, from his head to his foot,
And his clothes were all tarnished with ashes and soot;

A bundle of toys he had flung on his back,
    And he looked like a pedlar just opening his pack.

His eyes — how they twinkled!
    his dimples how merry!
His cheeks were like roses,
    his nose like a cherry!
His droll little mouth
    was drawn up like a bow,
And the beard on his chin
    was as white as the snow;
The stump of a pipe
    he held tight in his teeth,
And the smoke it encircled
    his head like a wreath;

He had a broad face and a little round belly,
That shook when he laughed,
like a bowlful of jelly.

He was chubby and plump – a right jolly old elf –
And I laughed when I saw him, in spite of myself.

A wink of his eye and a twist of his head
　　Soon gave me to know I had nothing to dread.
He spoke not a word,
　　but went straight to his work,

And filled all the stockings; then turned with a jerk,

And laying his finger aside of his nose,
And giving a nod, up the chimney he rose;

He sprang to his sleigh,
        to his team gave a whistle,

And away they all flew
  like the down of a thistle.

But I heard him exclaim,
  ere he drove out of sight,

"Happy Christmas to all,
and to all a good night!"